T0198404

I CAN DO IT, I WANT TO FLY!

By Jeremy Jones

Archway Publishing books may be ordered through booksellers or by contacting:

Archway Publishing
1663 Liberty Drive
Bloomington, IN 47403
www.archwaypublishing.com
844-669-3957

Scripture taken from the New King James Version. Copyright © 1982 by Thomas Nelson, Inc. Used by permission. All rights reserved.

ISBN: 978-1-6657-4266-5 (sc)
978-1-6657-4267-2 (e)

Library of Congress Control Number: 2023907396

Print information available on the last page.

Archway Publishing rev. date: 05/15/2023

I would like to dedicate this story to Jack, Carter, Ronin and Jasper.

"I CAN DO IT, I WANT TO FLY!"

started out as one of the bedtime stories I would tell my youngest son. It evolved over time and became a lesson on the power of the words can or can't. There were times the story was shorter than the previous time I told it and times I would elaborate details depending on how enthused I was about story time. As a busy Dad, I looked forward to this time of night. I hope this story helps empower your child with a lesson that can be applied in all phases of life.

On an early Spring Day in the park, two colorful birds met and fell in love.

They decided to build a nest high up in a tree made of grass, twigs, leaves and a few bubblegum wrappers.

Not long after, Mother bird laid 3 little speckled eggs.

Daddy bird kept the 3 little eggs warm,
while Mother bird went to get some tasty worms to eat.

Before too long, the 3 little eggs had hatched.

Mommy bird brought home some juicy worms to feed the baby birds.

7

Eagerly, Daddy bird flew around the nest and said,
"This is how we fly, we flap our wings and let the wind carry us".

The first little birdy said,
"I can do it, I want to fly".

The second little birdy said,
"I can do it,
but I don't want to fly".

The third little birdy said,
"I can't do it,
I don't want to fly".

Just then, Mommy bird flew in
with some yummy worms and said,
"Everyone must learn to fly so they
can get their own worms someday".

A few weeks later the 3 little birdies grew so much, they were pushing each other around in the nest.

So, Daddy bird flew around in circles and said,
"This is how we fly, we flap our wings and let the wind carry us".

The first little birdy said, "I can do it, I want to fly".

The second little birdy said, "I can do it, but I don't want to fly".

The third little birdy said, "I can't do it, I don't want to fly".

Again, Mommy bird flew in with some yummy worms.

"Everyone must learn to fly so they can get their own worms someday", she said.

By the end of Spring, the 3 little birdies had grown so much they were almost pushing each other out of the nest.

That day, Daddy bird said,
"Alright, today is the day everyone learns
how to fly so we can all get our own worms".

"Which of you little birdies would like to go first?",
Mommy bird asks.

The first little birdy said, "I can do it, I want to fly" and he flapped his wings and took off into the air.

The second little birdy said,
"I can do it, but I don't want to fly",
then the little birdy fell out of the
nest and flew away.

The third little birdy said,
"I can't do it, but I don't want to fly",
but he fell out of the nest and
started falling to the ground.

Just before the little birdy was about to hit the ground he said,
"I can do it, I want to fly", and he flapped his wings and flew away.

Then they all flew away together to get some delicious worms together.

Printed in the United States
by Baker & Taylor Publisher Services